FOR ANDERS

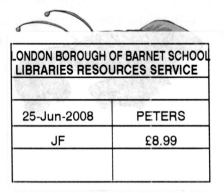

First published in 2008 by Orchard Books
First paperback publication in 2009

ORCHARD BOOKS
338 Euston Road, London NW1 3BH
Orchard Books Australia
Level 17/207 Kent St, Sydney, NSW 2000

ISBN 978 1 84616 722 5 (hardback)
ISBN 978 1 84616 730 0 (paperback)

A CIP catalogue record for this book is available from the British Library.

1 3 5 7 9 10 8 6 4 2 (hardback)
1 3 5 7 9 10 8 6 4 2 (paperback)

Printed and bound in Great Britain by
Antony Rowe Ltd, Chippenham, Wiltshire

Orchard Books is a division of Hachette Children's Books,
an Hachette Livre UK company.

www.hachettelivre.co.uk

VIKING VIK

AND THE CHARIOT RACE

SHOO RAYNER

ORCHARD BOOKS

Wulf grabbed
Gnasher by the
horns and pulled
with all his
might. "Will you
get a move on,
you stupid goat!"

"You'll never
get up the
mountain like
that," Vik sighed.
"Animals won't
do anything for
you if you treat
them badly."

Vik calmly led his goat, Curly, up the narrow mountain path. Between them they pulled and pushed their heavy cartload of supplies.

"Come on, you dimwit!" Wulf tugged at Gnasher's horns again, but Gnasher stood his ground and would not budge.

"You need to work as a team," Freya puffed, as she struggled up the path behind them. "Poor old Gnasher. You have to be gentle with him." Freya scratched the goat's forehead.

Gnasher bleated with joy and gave her a huge, friendly lick.

"Will you *come on!*"
Wulf yelled at the goat.
Gnasher bowed his head
and pawed the ground.

"You'd better
watch out," Vik
warned. "He looks
really angry!"

Gnasher lowered his
head, shook his horns,
took aim at Wulf's
bottom and charged.

"Get away from me, you stupid
animal!" Wulf scrambled up the
steep path as fast as he could go,
but Gnasher's eyes were fixed on
the target. He was determined to
get his own back on Wulf.

Vik's dog, Flek, thought it was a game. He joined in, yapping and chasing Wulf up the path.

"Whoa there!" Vik grabbed
Gnasher's reins and pulled him to a stop
before everything fell out of the cart.

"It's not a race, you know.
If you go too fast you'll fall
off the mountain."

13

It was true. The path was steep and dangerously close to the edge of the mountainside. One careless step could mean instant death for any of them.

"I hate goats!"
Wulf muttered
under his breath.

SUMMER PASTURES

Northern summers have
very long days, so the grass
grows green and lush in the
mountains, especially in
the lower meadows.

In the dark winter months,
goats eat hay made from
the summer grass.

"Look! There they are!" Freya pointed across the large green meadow, to where a herd of goats grazed in the long grass.

When Gnasher and Curly saw their girlfriends, they bleated at the tops of their voices and hurtled across the meadow to meet them. They didn't need to be told where to go!

The three children raced after them. The air filled with the sound of goat greetings and Flek barking. Soon the carts were unloaded and their supplies were stored away in the summer hut.

Being so early in the season, there wasn't anything for the children to take home, so after Edda the head goat girl had given them something to eat, they rounded up the goats and got ready for the journey back down the mountain.

MILKING GOATS AND MAKING CHEESE

Yes, you really can get milk from goats!

Viking goat's cheese is called "geitost". It is dark brown and tastes sweet, a bit like caramel toffee.

Wulf put some stones in his pocket.
When Vik wasn't looking, he grabbed
hold of Curly's reins and jumped into
Vik's cart. He slapped the reins hard
and set the goat off at a furious pace.

"Race you!" Wulf yelled, as Curly tore off down the winding, twisting mountain path.

"That's my cart!"
Vik shouted.

"I know!" Wulf
laughed, as clouds of
dust billowed out
behind him. "You
don't think I'd trust
that stupid old
Gnasher, do you?"

"You'd better get after him," Freya
said, anxiously. "He's going to hurt
himself if he's not careful."

Vik leapt into the other cart and snapped the reins. "Come on, Gnasher," he urged. "Let's get after them!"

The cart shook and rattled as they chased after Wulf and Curly. Flek ran alongside, barking with joy.

"Stop, you idiot!" Vik yelled. "You're going to kill yourself!"

"Never!" Wulf shouted back. "Last one home is a wet-legged lobster!"

Vik could hardly believe what was
happening. The steep mountainside
fell away at the edge of the path.
One false move and he could be
hurtling to his doom.

Vik spoke encouraging words to
Gnasher, trusting the animal to keep
him safely on the path.

He was catching Wulf up, but the
path was too narrow to overtake. Just up
ahead, the ground widened into a flat
expanse of rock. Vik urged Gnasher on.
The wheels of his cart clattered and
boomed on the rocky ground.

"I sound like Thor, riding
his chariot of thunder," Vik
thought to himself.

THOR AND HIS GOAT CHARIOT

When the great god, Thor, rides his chariot across the sky, he makes thunderstorms.

Magic goats called Tanngrisnir and Tanngnjóstr pull his chariot. Thor can cook them, eat them and bring them back to life again!

Wulf was thinking the same thing as he streaked along. He pulled the stones from his pockets and hurled them at Vik's wheels. "Here's a thunderbolt for you!" he taunted.

Gnasher screamed an awful bleat of
alarm, then, splaying his feet in front
of him, he skidded to a dead halt.
The worn leather harness snapped under
the strain as Vik and the cart tumbled
over and over on the hard, rocky ground.

When Curly heard
the crash behind him,
he slammed on the
brakes as well. Wulf
wasn't ready for it.
He flew right over
Curly's horns and
landed heavily in a
prickly juniper tree.

There wasn't a
bone in Vik's body
that didn't ache.
He picked himself up
and looked around.
His eyes throbbed.
Everything looked
blurred.

He shook his head to make
his eyes focus. Someone was
calling his name.

"Vik! Vik! Are you all right?" Freya ran down the path behind him. Now he could see her worried face.

"I — I think I'm OK," Vik stammered. "It hurts if I laugh, though."

"It's not a joking matter!" Freya snapped. "What about Wulf? Is he OK?"

Vik sat up and surveyed the damage.
His cart was smashed beyond repair.
Gnasher was consoling Curly, who was
still strapped to the other cart.

But where was Wulf?

"OW-OW-OWW!"

A long, painful
wail drifted out
from a juniper
tree nearby.

Wulf untangled himself from the
sharp, spiky branches. "Ow-ow-oww!
I prickle all over," he complained.
Gnasher saw him and began to
paw the ground.

"Watch out, Wulf!" Vik called. "Gnasher's looking angry again."

Wulf turned round in time to see Gnasher begin his charge. Wulf's face was bright red from all the prickles. It got redder still as he ran for his life.

Gnasher was much faster without a cart to pull. And Wulf's bottom was still his target. The distance closed between them. With one almighty butt from his horns, Gnasher sent Wulf flying over the side of the mountain.

Vik and Freya raced to the edge, fearing the worst. What awful sight would meet their eyes?

Each wondered how they would explain this terrible catastrophe when they got home…

Wulf was struggling and splashing about in a pool of clear blue water. A waterfall of melted snow crashed into the pool nearby.

Flek still thought it was a game. He leapt into the pool and joined Wulf in all the fun.

"Help! Get me out, it's f-f-f-freezing!" Wulf yelled.

Vik led Curly and the cart down the path, while Freya followed behind holding Gnasher's reins. Wulf dawdled some distance behind them.

His hands were as cold and blue as a live lobster...

...and his face was as hot and red as a cooked one.

His wet, woollen trousers
hung round his knees, making
him walk as though he needed
to go to the toilet.

"What was that you said about the last one home?" Vik called to Wulf. Freya covered her mouth, trying not to laugh.

"Something about wet-legged lobsters, wasn't it?" Vik taunted.

Wulf's soggy boots slapped wetly across the rock as he muttered curses about Vik and goats and lobsters under his breath.

Gnasher stopped to look at Wulf and bleated joyfully.

"This is not a laughing matter!" Vik told the goat, sternly. But Vik's eyes twinkled as a huge grin spread across his face.

Shoo Rayner

All priced at £8.99

The Viking Vik stories are available from all good bookshops,
or can be ordered direct from the publisher:
Orchard Books, PO BOX 29, Douglas IM99 1BQ
Credit card orders please telephone 01624 836000
or fax 01624 837033 or visit our internet site: www.orchardbooks.co.uk
or e-mail: bookshop@enterprise.net for details.

To order please quote title, author and ISBN
and your full name and address.
Cheques and postal orders should be made payable to 'Bookpost plc.'
Postage and packing is FREE within the UK
(overseas customers should add £2.00 per book).

Prices and availability are subject to change.